Modern Curriculum Press

BEGINNING
TO
READ
Series

SEASHELL MAGIC

by
Phylliss Adams
Carole P. Mitchener
Virginia Johnson

Illustrated by The Art & Design Co.

Library of Congress Cataloging-in-Publication Data

Adams, Phylliss.
  Seashell magic.

  Summary: Jason, Matt, and their classmates discover a
surprising thing about a seashell and learn that sound is created
by vibrations.
  [1. Shells—Fiction. 2. Sound—Fiction. 3. Schools—
Fiction] I. Mitchener, Carol P., 1955–   . II. Johnson,
Virginia, 1933–   . III. Art & Design Co. IV. Title.
PZ7.A21758Se 1987   [Fic]   87–18497
ISBN 0–8136–5191–3
ISBN 0–8136–5691–5 (pbk.)

 MODERN CURRICULUM PRESS

A Division of Simon & Schuster
13900 Prospect Road, Cleveland, Ohio 44136

The children had waited all day to
find out what was in the big white box.
"It's a surprise," laughed Miss Dee.
"But I'll show it to you after gym
this afternoon."

5

Now gym class was over.
And the children were coming back
in the room.
"Hey, everyone," yelled Jason,
"Sit down and stop talking so we
can see the surprise."

Miss Dee put the white box on the
   floor.
"This summer I went on a trip," she
   said,
"And I brought back a surprise for you.
I brought back part of the ocean."
"Part of the ocean!" giggled Matt.
"I bet it's a jar of salt water."

Surprise
Box

"That's a good guess," said Miss Dee,
"But it's not a jar of salt water."
"My dad once brought me a starfish,"
said Alice. "Is it a starfish?"

"Another good guess," said Miss Dee,
"But it's not a starfish.
I'll give you all a hint.
It's shaped something like your ears.
And it does something your ears do."

Everyone looked puzzled.
All at once Jason cried out,
"Is it a seashell?"
"Let's find out if Jason is right,"
said Miss Dee.
She took the lid off the box.

"A seashell!" cried the children.
"It is shaped like our ears,"
laughed Matt.

11

"But I don't get it," said Jason.
"You said you brought back part
of the ocean.
Why did you say that?"

Miss Dee smiled.
"Jason, hold the seashell up to
   your ear.
   What do you hear?"

"WOW!" cried Jason.
"It's roaring!
Just like the noise of the ocean!"

"Can I hear it?" asked Rosa.
"Me too," shouted all the children.
"Everyone must be quiet," said Miss
    Dee.
"We'll pass the seashell around
so all of us can hear it."

15

"But there's no water in the shell,"
said Matt.
"So why do we hear the ocean?"
"You don't," said Miss Dee.
"You hear a noise like the ocean.
Sound is made when something vibrates
or moves again and again and again."

"Is something vibrating inside
the shell?" asked Alice.
"Yes," said Miss Dee.
"The shell catches all the sounds
around it, just like your ears do."

"A magic shell!" said Alice.
"Not really," laughed Miss Dee.
"The sounds caught in the shell
make the air inside the shell vibrate.
And you hear a roaring sound like the
    ocean."

Jason giggled.
"What's so funny, Jason?" asked
    Miss Dee.
"You said our ears catch sounds.
That's funny!"

Sounds We Heard

someone shouting

a car horn

someone whistling

a door squeak

footsteps

laughing

a lawn mow

a sneeze

Miss Dee smiled.
"It does seem strange," she said.
"But our ears do catch sounds.
Let's all be very quiet.
Listen for all the sounds your ears
    catch."

Everyone was very quiet.
They listened for sounds.
What a lot of sounds they heard!
Miss Dee listed them all on the board.

"Is something vibrating when we talk?"
asked Rosa.
"Let's find out," said Miss Dee.
"Everyone put your hand on your
        throat.
Just like this.
Then say, 'Hello, Hello, Hello.' "

"I'm vibrating inside!" cried Matt.
"You all were," laughed Miss Dee.
"Your vocal cords were vibrating
inside your throat.
You can feel them vibrating.
But you can't see them."

23

"Can we see things vibrate?" asked
    Jason.
"Some things," said Miss Dee.
"I'll show you something I can
make vibrate."
Miss Dee picked up her guitar and
plucked on the strings.
"They're vibrating!" cried Jason.

"Can we hunt for things in the room
we can make vibrate?" asked Rosa.
"We don't have time now," said Miss Dee.
She pointed to the clock.
"But I want you to do something
tonight at home."

"Look for something you can make
vibrate to make a sound," said Miss Dee.
"Bring one thing you find to school
tomorrow for the surprise box."
"Can Matt and I bring something
together?" asked Jason.
"Sure," laughed Miss Dee.

"What can we find to take to school tomorrow?" asked Matt.
"Not that loud truck," laughed Jason.
"Or that big dog," giggled Matt.
"They won't fit in the surprise box."
"Let's start looking at my house," said Jason.

Matt called his mom to see if he could
stop at Jason's house.
His mom said it was alright.
So Matt and Jason started looking
for things that vibrate to make a sound.
What do you think they found?
You decide by choosing the ending:
Ending 1: Go to page 29.
Ending 2: Go to page 30.
Ending 3: Go to page 31.

Matt and Jason looked on top of the desk.
"Look at the ruler!" cried Jason.
"Can we make it vibrate to make a
    sound?"
They tried it and it worked!
So that is what they took to school!

Matt and Jason opened the desk drawer.
"Look at those rubber bands," cried
Matt.
"Can we make a rubber band vibrate
to make a sound?"
They tried it and it worked!
So that is what they took to school.

Ending 3

Matt and Jason looked in the toybox.
"Look at that old slinky," cried Jason.
"Can we make it vibrate to make a
   sound?"
They tried it and it worked!
So that is what they took to school.